Natalie

and the Bestest Friend Race

Natalie

and the Bestest Friend Race

Dandi Daley Mackall

ZONDER**kidz**

ZONDERVAN.com/
AUTHORTRACKER
follow your favorite authors

We want to hear from you. Please send your comments about this book
to us in care of zreview@zondervan.com.

For Ellie Hendren, with very much love.
That's what! ❀

Zonderkidz

Natalie and the Bestest Friend Race
Copyright © 2009 by Dandi Daley Mackall
Illustrations © 2009 by Lys Blakeslee

Requests for information should be addressed to:
Zonderkidz, *Grand Rapids, Michigan 49530*

Library of Congress Cataloging-in-Publication Data

Mackall, Dandi Daley.
    Natalie and the bestest friend race / by Dandi Daley Mackall ; [Lys Blakeslee,
illustrator].
        p. cm. -- (That's Nat! ; bk. 5)
    Summary: When Natalie accidentally reveals her best friend's secret, it
causes the friends to have their first real fight.
    ISBN 978-0-310-71570-2 (softcover)
    [1. Best friends--Fiction. 2. Friendship--Fiction. 3. Dyslexia--Fiction. 4. Chris-
tian life--Fiction.] I. Blakeslee, Lys, 1985- ill. II. Title.
    PZ7.M1905Nab 2009
    [Fic]--dc22   2008049736

Zonderkidz is a trademark of Zondervan

Editor: Betsy Flikkema
Art direction and design: Merit Kathan

Printed in the United States of America

10 11 12 13 14 15 /DCI/ 9 8 7 6 5 4 3

Table of Contents

Chapter 1

Me First!

"Me first!"

"*Me* first!"

Laurie and Sasha holler this at the same exactly time. Laurie is my bestest friend who is a girl. And Sasha is not.

In case you don't know this already, my name is Natalie 24. My friends, like Laurie, can call me Nat. Only not Sasha. Plus, my other middle name is Elizabeth. Only I don't like that one on account of you can get teased and called Lizard Breath if you're not careful.

I am running as hard as I can to the swings. But it's not hard enough.

"You lose again, Natalie!" Sasha shouts.

"Sorry, Nat," Laurie says. "I wasn't fast enough to save you a swing. You can have mine soon as I'm done."

There's another swing, but a girl from the other kindergarten class is sitting on it. Their class always gets out to recess first, some of the times.

"That's okay," I tell my best friend 'cause I don't want her to feel bad. "I like to watch." Only watching is boring. As soon as a swing is empty, I will fill it with me.

Sasha turns her back on me and says to Laurie, "You're a pretty fast runner."

"So are you," Laurie says back.

"I know," Sasha agrees.

"I guess I have to be fast around our house or I'd never get to the bathroom before Brianna hogs it," Laurie explains.

I laugh 'cause I know this is a true thing. Laurie's big sister is a bathroom-hogging girl.

Laurie makes a smiley face at me 'cause she knows I know about Brianna.

"Laurie," Sasha says, acting like I'm not here. "I hope we get to be on the same team in Kindergarten Olympics."

"In what?" I ask. "I never heard about Kindergarten Olympics."

Sasha keeps herself backwards to me, like Laurie is the only kid on this playground and Laurie is the one who asked about the Olympics and not me. "Oops. I'm not supposed to tell," Sasha says.

"Tell what?" Laurie demands.

"*I* know all about the Kindergarten Olympics because my mother is a volunteer parent. She's in charge of everything. I'm not supposed to tell anybody about it. But I guess I can tell you. Only you have to promise not to tell anybody else."

Laurie shrugs up her shoulders. She doesn't promise anything. That's what.

I shrug up my shoulders too. Only Sasha's back of the head doesn't see me do this.

Sasha goes on anyway. "Okay. We'll have races and jumps and contests and trophies even."

"Cool!" I shout. I saw some Olympics on TV. And Daddy and I cheered for the team that goes by the name of USA. They ran in circles. And other USA girls walked on boards and did tricks and jumped.

If I'm not a movie-star girl when I grow up, I might be an Olympic USA girl. I have very fast shoes. Sometimes. Sort of.

Sasha keeps talking to Laurie. "We should be on the same team, Laurie. We're both super fast."

Laurie leans around Sasha and gives me a great smile. "Nat, wouldn't it be cool to be on the same team? I can ask Sarah all about it."

Sarah is Laurie's old sister, who knows everything and doesn't hog bathrooms. Next year she can drive. Plus, she is mostly nice and wears lipstick.

"Hi, Farah!" Laurie calls, looking past me.

That's how I notice that Farah is standing behind me in the waiting-for-a-swing line. "Hi, Farah," I say too.

"Hello," Farah says back. She is a nice girl. Plus, she has aunts and uncles who live in other countries.

"Time to change swings," Laurie says. She hops off of hers and hands it to me.

Sasha hops off her swing. But she doesn't hand it over to Farah, so Farah has to grab the swing herself. It takes her two grabs.

By the time Farah sits on her swing, I'm already swinging. Her hair is so long she has to sweep it in front of her so she won't sit on it. I would love to wear Farah's hair. My hair is too short to sit on.

Farah and I try to get our swings to go up together and back together. Only this is harder than you think it's going to be.

Across the playground I hear a sound I usually love to hear. It's the sound of my bestest friend,

Laurie, laughing. Laurie's laughing sounds like jingly bells, ice cream, and the color purple all stirred up together. Plus angels.

Most of the time, I would stand on my head, or put a grasshopper on my nose, or tell one of my dad's silly jokes just to hear that laughing.

Only this is different.

Laurie is laughing at something without me.

And mixed in with Laurie's laugh is Sasha's laugh.

So maybe that's why that sound makes me stop swinging. And for the very first time since I started coming to this kindergarten place, I just wish recess would get over itself.

Chapter 2

Birds of a Feather

Our kindergarten teacher, who goes by the name of Miss Hines, is waiting for us when we come in from recess. She has spread out our reading blankets in the front, the back, and the side of our classroom.

We sit at our desks and wait for each other.

Then Miss Hines stands in front of her giant desk and shouts, "Time for reading groups!"

"Duh," Peter says.

Some kids laugh. Like Sasha. She stands up and starts toward the blanket where her group reads.

"Not yet, birds!" Miss Hines calls out.

Sasha, Peter, and Bethany have to sit down again.

"Since it's spring," Miss Hines begins, "the birds have been migrating, haven't they? I know I've seen large flocks of birds flying north."

This is a true thing about seeing flocks of birds. My granny and I saw a gazillion birds fly right over Frank, our big tree that lives in the backyard. And some of them took a time-out on Frank's branches.

"So," Miss Hines goes on, "let's all take our spots in our winter homes. Go ahead and sit in your regular reading groups. Red Birds! Blue Birds! Robins! You know where to go."

Laurie and I go to the blanket in the back of our classroom. We are Robins. I wanted to be a Purple Bird, but our teacher said we don't have any.

"Our books aren't here, Miss Hines!" Sasha yells

from the side of our classroom. She's in the Blue Bird group, with Peter.

"Be patient, my little birdies," Miss Hines says.

When we're all sitting in our bird-group circles, Miss Hines says, "It's time for birds to migrate to their summer homes."

"I knew it," Laurie whispers to herself.

"Knew what?" I whisper.

I don't think she hears me 'cause she just keeps staring at Miss Hines.

"The birds you've watched flying north aren't the only birds on the move!" Miss Hines has on her cheerleader voice. "You reading birds are on the move too! All new groups, all new birds. Won't that be fun?"

I think it sounds fun. 'Sides, I'm tired of being a Robin. "I hope we're owls," I whisper to Laurie.

"They never do owls," Laurie says. She knows things on account of Sarah and Brianna already did kindergarten. Laurie is still staring at our teacher. Plus also, Laurie is sucking in her lips, which is how my bestest friend does thinking. And sometimes worrying.

Maybe Laurie is doing worrying 'cause she likes robins and wants to stay being one.

"What do you hope we are?" I ask Laurie.

Laurie doesn't answer. Maybe she didn't hear me on account of she was looking so hard at our teacher.

"So," Miss Hines says in her cheerleading voice, "good-bye Blue Birds, Red Birds, and Robins! Hello, Goldfinches!" She points to the old Red Bird group in the front of the room. "Bethany, Jason, and Farah, you birds come stand by me for a minute, okay?"

"Oh, no," Laurie whispers.

"What?" I watch Bethany, Jason, and Farah move to our teacher. Jason hops on one foot and flaps his elbows like a hurt bird.

"I knew it," Laurie says.

Now I'm doing worrying too. "Knew *what*?" I ask her. "What's Miss Hines doing with them?" I whisper. Jason is my bestest friend who is a boy, and Farah is maybe my second best friend who is a girl. Plus, Bethany is in my Sunday school class.

"She's mixing up our groups." Laurie sounds chokey.

"You mean she might take us apart?" I ask. "And put us back together again with you and me in different groups?"

Laurie nods. I think I see tears leaking out of one eye.

It would be a very bad thing to be stuck in a group without Laurie, on account of I love being in reading group with her. But I don't think it would

be a crying thing. 'Sides, we hardly even got to talk without getting yelled at when we were Robins.

I start to tell Laurie this, but she puts up her hand, like our moms do to shush us.

Miss Hines gives our group a big smiley face. "Instead of the Robins, on this reading blanket will be the home of the Mockingbirds."

She turns her smiley face to the side of our classroom. "Over there, instead of Blue Birds, we'll have Woodpeckers. So, we have Goldfinches, Mockingbirds, and Woodpeckers."

"I never saw a mockingbird. What do they look like?" I ask Laurie.

She doesn't seem to hear me again.

Miss Hines smiles over at our group. "Anna and Matthew, would you please trade places with Griff and Lisa?"

They trade places and bird groups.

"Okay. Now, Bethany, Jason, and Farah, go to the Mockingbirds. And Eric, Laurie, and Chase, come to the Goldfinch group."

Laurie gasps. "I knew it," she whispers.

And this time I see tears leaking out of her eyes.

Chapter 3

Homework

"Don't be sad, Laurie," I say. On account of her sad makes me sad. "I'll only be a little away from you."

Laurie doesn't even look at me. She stares at her shoes. Then she gets up and shuffles to the Goldfinch group.

Jason and Farah and Bethany come to the Robins, which is now the Mockingbird group. I am wondering how real birds can keep this stuff straight in their tiny heads.

Jason plops next to me, where Laurie was sitting. "Hey, Teacher!" Jason never says "Miss Hines." "Hey, Teacher! Our group wants to be Cuckoo!" he shouts.

"Your group *is* cuckoo!" Peter shouts back. He and Sasha are Woodpeckers. Sasha laughs way too loud at what Peter said.

I think Sasha's buddy, Peter the Not-So-Great, could also go by the name Peter the Not-So-Funny. That's what.

Miss Hines passes out reading books to all of us birds.

"I like this new bird name," Farah whispers. "Mockingbirds can sing two hundred songs."

"I didn't know there *were* that many songs," I admit.

Farah smiles without showing her teeth. "Many of the mockingbird's songs come from other birds, and even other animals and machines. They repeat the sounds they hear around them. My grandmother told me this."

"You are a very smart kindergarten girl," I tell Farah. And this is a true thing. My two best friends who are girls, Laurie and Farah, are the smartest kindergarten girls I know.

Farah grins. "I am glad to be in your group, Natalie."

I smile back at Farah. I've told her a gazillion times that she can call me Nat, like Laurie and Jason do.

I try to see if Laurie is still leaking tears. But she has her face down, and I can't tell.

When school is over, Laurie and I walk outside, where our moms pick us up.

"Want to come over to my house?" I ask Laurie. "My mom said it was okay if your mom says it's okay."

Laurie shakes her head in the no way.

This is a strange thing. Laurie loves coming over to my house. Her house has too many people in it.

"How come you can't come over?" I ask.

"I have homework," she answers.

"We don't have homework."

"I have reading homework," Laurie says.

"Goldfinches got homework?" Maybe it's a good thing I got to be a Mockingbird. I like school but not at home.

"There's Mom," Laurie says, taking off for her car. She really is a fast runner.

"Bye, Laurie!" I shout after her. "Call me later!"

"Nat! Over here!" My granny is waving her arms like she's showing airplanes where to land.

I run to Granny and give her a big, fat hug. "Granny! How come *you're* here?"

Granny hugs me back. "Can't I come pick up my

19

granddaughter when I've got a mind to? You think I'm too old for kindergarten?"

"Kinda," I admit. I love seeing my granny. But I look around for my mom, on account of she picks me up every day in Buddy. "Where's Mommy?"

"Your mother had a meeting."

"Again?"

"Again," Granny says. "I asked her if I could be the one to get you from school. You got a problem with that?" She grins at me. "Up for a walk? Too gorgeous to ride."

Granny and I walk. Plus also, we talk.

"Granny, guess what. I'm not a Robin anymore. I'm a Mockingbird."

"You are?" She looks down at me.

"Laurie is a Goldfinch. Only I don't think Laurie likes that bird."

"That so?" Granny says. We hold hands to cross the street. "Mockingbird, huh?" Granny says. "Never thought I'd have one of those for a granddaughter."

"Jason wanted to be a Cuckoo," I tell her.

Granny laughs her head off.

When we get home, we go straight to the kitchen. Percy, my cat, comes too. I get the bag of chocolate-chip cookies, and Granny pours the milk.

"Your mom said Laurie might come over this afternoon," Granny says.

"She has homework," I tell Granny. I feel sorry
for my bestest friend missing out on my granny and
cookies.

"Homework?" Granny says. "In kindergarten?"

"Reading homework," I explain.

"Do *you* have reading homework?" Granny asks.

"Nope. But I might read anyway. I like that
reading, Granny."

Granny gives me a big smiley face. "Me too.
Nothing better." My granny reads the Bible every
single day. She reads it so much that those pages
aren't stuck to the covers anymore.

We eat another cookie and dip it into our milk.
Laurie loves to do this trick. "Granny, can I call
Laurie and see if she can come over now? Maybe she
did her homework already."

"Good idea," Granny says. She hands me her cell

phone.

I push the number eight button. Granny has my bestest friend's number in her phone. All you do is punch *8* to get it out. "Crazy eight," Granny calls it.

"Hello?"

I can tell two things by this *hello*: (1) This is Brianna, Laurie's not-so-nice sister, who is in the fifth grade. (2) Brianna is probably going to be not so nice when she finds out I'm the one calling.

"Hi," I say.

"Oh, it's you," Brianna says, like I should be somebody she likes better than me. "Just a minute." Away from the phone, she shouts, "Laurie! Your annoying friend is on the phone!"

I wait a gazillion minutes. Then Brianna comes back. "Laurie says she's busy. Homework."

"Still?" I ask.

Only Brianna already clunked the phone off.

Chapter 4

'Slexia

Granny and I put three puzzles together. But I really want to play outside with my bestest friend. "Can I see if Laurie can come over yet?" I ask Granny.

She hands over her cell phone, and I punch crazy eight.

This time Sarah answers. "Hello?"

"Hi."

"Hi, Natalie." Sarah doesn't sound like she hates me for calling her sister. She is a very pretty and nice sister. "You're waiting to play with Laurie, aren't you?"

"Yeah."

"Well, I tell you what, Natalie," Sarah is talking at me like we are the same oldness and maybe friends. "I can't get that friend of yours to stop studying. Why don't you come over here and get her to go outside?"

I think this is a super idea. I never get to go to their house very much. "Okay! I'll be right there."

Granny walks with me to Laurie's house, which is on our street, only across one little street and up more.

Sarah is waiting at the door when we get there. "Laurie's still at it." She opens the screen door.

I tell Granny "bye" and walk on in.

Laurie is sitting at their eating table. Brianna is plopped on the couch, watching TV. And talking on the phone. Plus listening to music.

"Hi, Laurie!" I call to my bestest friend.

Laurie looks up from her reading book. "Hey, Nat. Sorry I couldn't come over."

"Are you still doing homework?" I ask.

"I'm trying," she says.

"You should tell Miss Hines it's not fair. We didn't have to do homework in the Mockingbirds. She's not playing fair with Goldfinches. That's what."

"Yeah," Laurie says.

"You shoulda stayed with me," I go on. "You shouldn't have changed groups."

Laurie's eyes turn to little lines. "Did I ask to change groups?" Her voice gets loud. "Did you see me ask to change groups, Nat?"

I shake my head. Laurie is a little bit scary.

"Did you see me ask if I could go and be a Goldfinch?" she demands. Before I can answer, she shouts, "No! I didn't! Nobody asked *me* if I wanted to be in a different reading group!"

I am so surprised, that I can't talk. Laurie never yelled at me before. I don't know what I did. But it must have been really bad to make her this mad. "I didn't mean it, Laurie." I just wish I knew what I didn't mean. So I wouldn't do it again.

Tears are leaking out of Laurie's eyes. She shoves her reading book away. "You didn't do anything. I'm sorry, Nat."

"Are you mad at me?" Tears are trying to leak out of me too. "'Cause maybe Miss Hines will let me be a Goldfinch. I could ask her."

Laurie's mouth tries to smile at me, but her eyes are still leaking. "Never mind, Nat." She stares down at a reading book page my Mockingbird group did today.

"Is that your homework?" I ask. "We did that one and the next page already."

Laurie slams the book shut. "Let's go outside and play."

I think this is a very good idea. "Cool!"

Laurie's backyard doesn't have swings like mine. Or Frank. But there are always fun things back here. Like a big hole. And a mole that digs tunnels.

We find a rusty silver baton in a stickery bush. "This was Bri's," Laurie says, knocking dirt out of it.

We take turns trying to twirl it until Brianna comes flying out of the house.

"That's my baton!" she screams. "Gimme that!" She grabs it out of Laurie's hand and twirls it. Only she's not so much better than we were.

Laurie's dad drives up. Then Sarah hollers out at us, "Natalie, your mom called. She'll be by to pick you up in a few minutes."

Laurie and I slow-walk in.

"This was fun, Laurie," I tell her. I'm already forgetting about the yelling part.

"Yeah," she says. Only her voice sounds frowny.

Inside, we sit at the table to wait for my mom. Brianna is sitting across from us. Her schoolbook is open, but she's just drawing hearts on a piece of paper.

"Is that your homework?" I ask her. On account of if it is, maybe homework isn't so hard in the fifth grade.

"Mind your own business," Brianna says.

Laurie opens her book to that page the Mockingbirds already did. She copies a word on a sheet of paper with many copied words on it. "Brianna, what's H-O-U-S-E?" Laurie spells those letters out loud.

Brianna doesn't even look. She keeps drawing her hearts all over the place.

"House," I answer. I know this on account of the Mockingbirds learned that word. "Only your *S* is turning funny. And your *E* is backwards." I pick up a pencil and draw those letters facing the right way.

"How come Goldfinches didn't do this page today at school?" I ask.

"Because Goldfinches are in the dumb group,"

Brianna says without looking up.

"Brianna!" Sarah snaps. She bursts to the table, bonks her sister on the head, and sits down with us. "What's the matter with you, Bri?"

Brianna shrugs and keeps drawing.

"She's right," Laurie whispers.

"No she's not!" I shout. "There aren't any dumb groups in our kindergarten. Miss Hines says we are her smartest-ever class." This is a true thing. She has said this to us many times.

Brianna snickers. "Did she give you the bit about the birds? How it's time to migrate to your summer homes?"

"Yes." I am amazed that Brianna knows this.

Laurie is drawing snakes on the paper with her backwards *S*. "I'm in the group with all the kids who can't read. The dumb group. So I'm dumb."

"No, sir!" I shout. "You're the smartest kid I know. You know more stuff than me about everything. Plus also, you are the best colorer in our whole entire class. That's what!"

"If I'm so smart, then why did I get moved to the dumb group today?" Laurie asks.

"It's not a dumb group." Sarah scoots closer to Laurie. "I was in that group. I ought to know."

"You were in the du — ?" I stop before that

"dumb" word makes it out of my mouth.

"Everybody learns to read at a different pace," Sarah says. "Some of us, like Laurie and me, take our time."

I turn to Brianna. "Did you take your time in that group?"

"Not me," Brianna says.

"Bri also missed out on the good looks in the family," Sarah says. "Right, Laurie?"

Laurie doesn't answer.

I smile at Sarah. She's right. She and Laurie are both full of beautifulness.

"At least I don't write backward," Brianna mutters.

I glance at Laurie's backwards letters. "Do *you* write backwards?" I ask Sarah.

"I used to. Sometimes. Not now. Reading used to be hard for me too. Now I read more than anybody in this house. I love to read. Laurie will get the hang of it. It's just harder for her than it is for you."

"But why is it harder?" I ask.

Brianna blurts out the answer, "She probably has dyslexia."

'Slexia? This word makes my neck chokey and my stomach twisty. "What did you say?"

"Dys-lex-i-a!" Brianna shouts.

I look at Laurie, hoping she'll shout back, "I do not!"

Instead, she mumbles, "It's true."

I cannot believe this true thing. My bestest friend in the whole world has 'slexia.

Tears make my eyes burny. "Laurie?" My voice is crackly on account of tears are leaking in my neck too. "Are…are you going to die?"

Chapter 5

My Mistake

Brianna busts up laughing.

"Stop laughing!" I shout. "I can't believe you don't even care about your own sister. My bestest friend."

"And I can't believe you thought she'd die from dyslexia," Brianna says. She's still laughing hard. "You better tell your teacher to bump you down to the dumb group too, Natalie."

"Laurie's not dying," Sarah says. She puts her hand on my hand. It makes my neck not so much chokey. "Dyslexia is a learning disability. That's all. Mom has it too. Our brains connect sounds and letters different than most people's brains." She grins

at Laurie. "But we do have great brains."

"Maybe Jason has it." I'm remembering something about my other bestest friend, the one who is a boy. "He turned his *S* backwards before Miss Hines showed him frontwards."

"I doubt it," Sarah says. "Lots of kids your age get letters backward and don't have dyslexia. But it's different with Laurie. She doesn't see the letters the same way."

This does not seem like a fair thing. And right then, right there, I whisper this to God. I hope it doesn't hurt God's feelings, but I tell him I don't like that he let Laurie have 'slexia. And that Brianna calls her dumb. And I wish he hadn't made that mistake with my friend. That's what.

Laurie looks even sadder than she did at school.

"Does Miss Hines know?" I ask.

Laurie nods. "She called up my mom first. Then we all met after school last week."

"You didn't tell me." Best friends are supposed to tell everything to each other.

Laurie makes her eyes little at me. "And you can't tell anybody at school, Nat. Not even Jason."

"Okay." Only I still think she should have told me.

"I mean it, Nat," Laurie says. "I don't want

anybody to know."

"Natalie?" Laurie's mom calls. "Your grandmother is here for you."

"Granny?" I get up and go to the front door, and there is my granny. "I'll be right there," I shout.

I run back to my friend and hug her. There are many things I want to say to her. Only I don't know what they are.

"Bye," I say.

"Bye," she says.

Granny and I walk outside together.

"Where's Mommy? Why isn't she here to get me? Is she still at the meeting?"

"No, she's home." Granny takes my hand and holds it. I can feel her finger bones. "It's such a gorgeous day. I wanted to walk over and fetch you myself. You got a problem with that?"

"No." I watch my feet while we walk and make sure I don't step on any cracks. I don't want to break my mommy's back. I think about Laurie's mom and that she has 'slexia too. And that makes me sadder.

"What's the matter, honey?" Granny asks.

My granny can always tell when there's a matter. Sooner or later, I always end up telling her what that matter is.

So I vote *sooner*. "Granny, Laurie has a terrible

disease."

"What? Are you sure?"

"I just found out. My bestest friend has 'slexia."

Granny gets very big in her eyes. "Slexia?"

I want to explain it to my granny. Only I can't think of the words Sarah used. "That's when you read backwards and your mom and sister have it too."

"Do you mean *dyslexia*?" Granny asks.

"Yeah."

Granny lets out air like she was holding her breath.

"And our teacher moved Laurie to the dumb reading group on account of it."

"Nat, don't call it dumb, you hear? And if any of those other kids call it a dumb group, you set them straight! You know good and well how smart that friend of yours is."

"That's what I told her. She shouldn't be in that ...that group Miss Hines moved her to."

"None of those kids in that group are dumb," Granny says. "They're all smart. And they're all God's creations."

"Then why did God give Laurie 'slexia? How come God made that mistake with my best friend?"

Granny stops walking. She stares down at me until I look up at her. Her eyes are not little lines. She is not aggravated. But she has thinking wrinkles on her head, like she's going to say something really important.

"Natalie 24, God doesn't make mistakes."

"But—"

"No sir," Granny says, not letting me say anything. "That's where you start. God does not make mistakes. No buts there."

I think about this. "Okay. Then why does Laurie have it?"

Granny starts us walking again. "Now that's a harder question." We walk some more. "I've talked this over with God a lot, Nat, why some people are so sick and others can't walk or talk or maybe do have horrible diseases."

"What does God say?" I want to know this answer.

"I don't think we'll get the whole answer until we're in heaven and can ask God face-to-face. But I've come up with part of an answer."

Part is more than I've got. "Like what?"

"Well, when Adam sinned, the whole earth fell with him. That's where we get weeds. The garden of Eden didn't have any before. But now we've got weeds, and we've got disease, and even dyslexia. So sometimes, things just happen, honey. Weeds grow. Diseases come."

I know about Adam and Eve being bad in that garden. So this kind of makes sense. Only not so much in my head. "I wish it didn't happen to Laurie."

"Laurie will be just fine. You know, she might even end up a better person with dyslexia than she would have been without it. And you might be a better person knowing her, with her having dyslexia. You wouldn't change your friend, would you? You like Laurie the way she is?"

"She's my bestest friend in the whole world! I would never change her."

Granny nods. "And I guarantee you this: God is right there with her, helping her through it."

Thinking about Jesus sitting beside Laurie, even

when she makes *S* backwards, makes me feel better. Only not all the way. "Granny, I'm not sure I get it all the way," I admit.

"Well, join the club, Nat. But don't forget. God gets it all the way. And he doesn't make mistakes."

Chapter 6

Questions and Answers

Mommy is in the kitchen putting dinner in the microwave. I run up and hug her hard. On account of it feels like I didn't see her for so long.

She hugs me back. "How was school today, Nat?"

"First, it was okay. Jason stuck his finger in Ham the Hamster's cage and acted like he got bit. Only he didn't. And Miss Hines told him not to cry about wolves. And Anna lost her tooth—this one right here—only hers. Plus, Sasha said she already lost all of her teeth. But then we were birds, only different birds with different homes. And Laurie isn't a Mockingbird. She's a Goldfinch, and that made her really sad. Only it's not a dumb group, on account of she's so very smart and so are all of God's creations 'cause God doesn't make mistakes. Granny said so. Only I didn't ask her about cockroaches. 'Cause those guys sure don't look like God did that on purpose."

I have more stuff about my day, but Mom has to take things out of the microwave and put other things in there. This is how my mom cooks.

Granny goes to her home. Then Daddy comes

home for dinner. And I tell him all the stuff about
Laurie. So I only eat about four spaghetties 'cause
I'm not allowed to talk with food in my mouth.

"Do you know about 'slexia, Daddy?" I eat a
spaghetti while he answers.

"I know what dyslexia is. A buddy of mine in
college had it, but he loved reading. He was a good
writer too. I think most people work their way
around it."

"Marge told me they were taking Laurie to see
someone about it," Mom says. Marge is Laurie's
mom.

"And you didn't tell me?" I say. "You should
have told me."

Mom knows Laurie's my best friend.

Mom is all done with her food. "If Laurie wanted you to know, Natalie, she would have told you. *I* didn't have the right to tell you. Marge talked to me in confidence."

I don't feel like eating. I push my plate away. I still think everybody should have told me.

Daddy and I go outside to play. Sometimes he is a good player.

"Want to race?" he asks.

And that makes my head remember. "Daddy! I forgot the other big news."

"What news is that?" Mom is coming outside too.

"We're going to have a Kindergarten Olympics, that's what!"

"Yeah?" Daddy says.

"Cool," Mom says. She sits on my swing.

I run over and sit on Laurie's swing. "Only we're not supposed to know about it yet."

"So why *do* you know about it?" Mom asks.

"Sasha's mother is in charge of the whole thing. And she told Sasha. And Sasha told us. Only really just Laurie. Only I heard. And Sasha said we're not supposed to tell."

"When is it, Nat?" Daddy asks. He tosses the ball in the air and swings at it. He misses. But he tries again.

"I don't know."

"What events?" Daddy tosses the ball, swings, and hits the ball. He is a good player all by himself.

"I don't know."

Mommy and Daddy have other questions about Kindergarten Olympics. Only I am all out of answers.

The next day at kindergarten, I get some of those answers.

"Class!" Miss Hines shouts. "I need you to quiet down. Jason, sit down! Bethany and Kate, no whispering."

This works pretty good and makes us quiet.

"I have an announcement," Miss Hines says.

This works even better, on account of we love

'nouncements. They are like surprises you don't know yet. Only I'm pretty sure I know this one.

I look over at Laurie, but Sasha is talking in Laurie's ear. And Sasha's big head is blocking the way.

"As part of the national health program, West Side Elementary will participate in this year's Kindergarten Olympics!" Miss Hines waits for us to be excited.

We are.

Jason jumps out of his desk and screams, "Yahoo! Me first!"

"Jason, sit down," Miss Hines says, only not mean.

"My mother is in charge of it," Sasha says without raising her hand.

"We have several parent volunteers who will be helping out with the different events," Miss Hines says.

"What events?" Peter asks. He looks more frowny faced than most of the boys in our class. Except for Brandon, who hates outside recess.

"I don't have the list, but we'll have relay races, hurdles, and other running events," Miss Hines explains.

"What if you do not want to run in a race?" Farah asks.

"Yeah," Brandon agrees.

"What's the matter, Brandon?" Peter has on his mean teasing voice. "Are you chicken?"

"No talking. Raise your hand if you have a question," Miss Hines says. "This will be fun, everybody! We'll divide into teams, and everyone will participate and get an Olympic T-shirt."

"Teacher! Teacher!" Jason waves his hand like it's on fire.

"Yes, Jason," Miss Hines says.

"How do you decide teams? Can we race to pick teams?" Jason stays in his scat, but his legs are running. His shoes are untied. "Or *jump* to pick teams?" He jumps up and crashes down in his seat again.

"We'll select two team captains, and the captains will choose their teams," our teacher explains.

Sometimes Laurie and I get out all of my stuffed animals and choose up sides. Only my one-eared rabbit always gets picked last. And that makes him sad.

I really hope my bestest friend, Laurie, and I get on the same team.

"Can I be a captain?" Peter asks.

"Me too!" yell a bunch of kids.

"We'll draw names for it." Miss Hines opens her

desk drawer and comes out with a small green plastic bowl. She tips it so we can see the pieces of paper in there. "I've written each of your names on a slip of paper and put them all into this bowl." She shakes the bowl.

"Okay. I'm going to close my eyes." Our teacher does this. "And I'll reach in and pull out a name." She does this too. Then she opens her eyes.

We are not bumbly bees. We are very quiet.

Miss Hines raises her eyebrows, and then reads the name on the paper: "Peter."

"Yes!" Peter punches the air with both hands. "All right! We're number one! We're number one! I am Peter the Great, and we are going to smash the other team and—"

"Sit down and be quiet, Peter," Miss Hines says in her not-kidding-around voice, "or I'll have to choose another captain."

That does it

for Peter. He sits down on the outside, but I can tell his insides are still cheering.

Miss Hines closes her eyes again and reaches into the bowl. She comes out with another piece of paper. Her smiley face is bigger than before. "Our second team captain is...Laurie."

I can't believe this lucky thing! My bestest friend who is a girl is a team captain.

Laurie turns in her desk and sends me her smiley face, right over Sasha's head.

And I know one big, fat answer. And that is for the question in my head: *Will Laurie and I get to be on the same team?* Now I know that answer: *Yes!*

Chapter 7

Whispers

I can't wait for recess to talk to Laurie. Only I have to. On account of there's no whispering in kindergarten. Sometimes.

"All right, birds," Miss Hines says. She is setting out our reading blankets for our three groups that are all smart. "Goldfinches, Woodpeckers, and Mockingbirds, fly to your summer homes."

We do.

I keep sneaking peeks at the Goldfinches. Laurie still looks sad.

My Mockingbird home is so close to the Woodpeckers that I can hear Peter bragging about who he's going to pick for his Olympic team.

"Hey!" Peter says with his mean laugh. "I should just pick our whole group to be on my team. Winners only in the smart group!"

Jason, my bestest friend who is a boy and also a Mockingbird, flaps his wings and scoots closer to the Woodpeckers. He whisper-shouts at Peter, "What do you mean, 'the smart group'?"

"*This* group!" Peter says, like Jason is a birdbrain for not knowing this. "*My* group. The Woodpeckers."

Jason flaps his wings harder. "Woodpeckers poke holes in trees. They're not smart. *Mockingbirds* are smart."

"Oh yeah?" Peter says. "What page are you on in the reading workbook?"

"I don't know," Jason says.

"We are on page ten," Farah tells him. She must hear Peter too, on account of he is a loud boy.

I look around to see why Miss Hines isn't yelling at Peter and Jason. Then I see our teacher in the way front of the room with the Goldfinches. Sometimes we get helpers to help all of the birds read at the same time. Only not today. Miss Hines has to take turns at birdhouses today.

"*We're* on page sixteen," Peter says.

"Yeah," Sasha says. She's a Woodpecker too, like Peter.

"And the dumb group probably hasn't even found page one yet," Peter says. Then he laughs his head off.

"Quiet down, Woodpeckers," Miss Hines calls. "I'll be over there in just a minute."

Only I can't wait just a minute. My heart is thumpy, on account of what that loud Peter said. I scoot closer to the Woodpeckers. "Peter!" I whisper-shout. "There's no such thing as a dumb group!"

Peter changes to a whispering boy. "Oh yeah? There is too. Ask your buddy Laurie. She ought to know. She's in that dumb group."

"She is not, Peter!"

Peter acts like he didn't hear this. "So that means she's dumb."

My hands turn into fists. I want to scream at Peter. Only it's against a big school law. "You be quiet, you…you…you Peter the Not-So-Great!" I whisper so hard at him that spit comes out.

"Well, she's Laurie the Not-So-Smart!" Peter spits back.

"Laurie *is* smart!" I whisper-spit.

"Yeah?" Peter whispers back. "So why is she in the dumb group then?"

"Because Laurie has 'slexia! That's what!" Those words spit out all by themselves. I didn't mean to say them.

It's all Peter's fault.

"Turn to page ten," Miss Hines says, showing up to work with us Mockingbirds.

I turn to page ten. And I try to read the words. Only I keep losing my place. On account of Peter made me so aggravated.

At lunchtime, Laurie and I get our matching purple lunch boxes out of our cubbies. We smiley face each other 'cause being lunch eaters is a gazillion times better than being birds today.

The lunchroom is filled with noises. I see Brianna, but she always pretends she doesn't see Laurie and me.

We sit at the same table at the back, where we always sit most of the time. I give Laurie half of my peanut butter sandwich. She gives me half of her cheese sandwich.

"I don't like picking sides for a team," Laurie says. "I don't want to make anybody feel bad."

"At least this way, you and I can be on the same team for sure," I point out.

"That's true," Laurie says. "Should we pick Sasha? She's really fast."

This is a true thing. "But she's also really Sasha."

"That's true," Laurie agrees.

We talk about more kids we could pick for our

team.

Peter shuffles by our table and stops right behind Laurie. "Oooh, better not get too close," he warns.

"Too close to what?" Eric asks him.

"Her." Peter points to Laurie. "Better be careful," he says, looking around our table at Farah, Anna, Bethany, and a girl from the other class.

The other-class girl looks scared. "How come?"

"'Cause it may be catching," Peter says.

My stomach is twitchy. Cheese is stuck in my neck.

Anna puts down her hot dog and frowns up at Peter. "What's catching?"

"You'll have to ask Laurie," Peter says.

Peanut butter is pushing on the cheese in my neck. They want out.

"Me? What are you talking about, Peter?" Laurie says. "Why don't you go bother somebody else?"

"Nobody else has what you have," Peter says.

I want to slap my hands over Peter's mouth. I want to shove him away from our table. I want to drag Laurie out of the lunchroom.

Only I can't move.

"You don't make any sense, Peter," Laurie says. She lifts her cheese sandwich for another bite. "So what do I have that nobody else has?"

The lunchroom stops. The noises stop. The air dries up.

And Peter says, "Dyslexia."

Chapter 8

Who Said That?

Laurie drops her cheese sandwich and runs for the bathroom.

I run after her.

She is standing at the faraway sink, crying.

Seeing her makes my stomach burn. I think my heart burns too. I walk over and stand beside my friend. Only I don't know what to say.

"I can't believe Peter said that!" Laurie cries.

"Me either!" I am so mad at Peter. He made Laurie cry.

"Why would he do that?"

"Because he's not nice!" I have never been this much mad at *anybody*!

Laurie's face is red and wet. Her curls are not bouncy. "But how did Peter know?"

"Huh?"

"Peter," Laurie says. "How did he know I have dyslexia?"

I am staring into my best friend's red eyes. I open my mouth, only words won't come out.

"Miss Hines knew," Laurie says.

"Our teacher would never tell Peter." I know this

is a true thing. And I wish I hadn't told Peter either. I didn't mean to. "Maybe it was an accident," I say. And this feels true.

"I know!" Laurie says. "Brianna. I'll bet Brianna told one of her friends. And word got back to Peter. How could Bri do that to me?"

"You don't—," I begin.

"Girls?" Somebody else's teacher sticks her head in. "Time to go back to your class. Come on now."

I pull down a paper towel and hand it to Laurie.

She takes it and wipes her face. "Thanks, Nat. I don't know what I'd do without you."

Laurie and I walk back to class together. We get all the way to our cubbies, when Laurie shouts, "We left our lunch boxes, Nat!"

Only when we look in our cubbies, our lunch boxes are already there.

"I'll bet Farah picked them up for us. Or Anna," I guess.

Peter comes up behind us. We act like we don't see him. He starts singing, "Here comes Queen Dyslexia! Here comes Queen Dyslexia!"

"You be quiet, Peter!" I shout.

"Queen what?" Jason asks, sticking something into his crammed-full cubby.

"Dyslexia," Peter says. "I have a cousin who has that. He's not very—"

"Peter!" Miss Hines storms out of nowhere. Her shoes *thunk-thunk* up to us. She leans down, face-to-face with Peter. "Apologize to Laurie right now!"

I have never seen our teacher so mad. I am mad right along with her.

Peter folds his arms in front of him, turns his eyes to lines, and doesn't say anything.

"You heard me, Peter," Miss Hines says. She is not shouting now. But I think she's even madder than before. "Tell Laurie you're sorry."

"Why should I?" Peter asks.

"Because you hurt Laurie's feelings," she answers.

"Yeah!" I say. I totally agree with our teacher. Peter hurt Laurie's feelings so much that tears came out.

"It's true," Peter says this with pouty lips. "She *does* have dyslexia."

"That doesn't matter," Miss Hines explains. "That's Laurie's information. Not yours. You have no right to make fun or tease or whatever you think you're doing by talking about something Laurie doesn't want to talk about. Apologize, Peter."

I think this is a great idea. Peter hurt my friend, and he better say sorry.

"That's not fair," Peter says. "How come *I* have to apologize? Make *Natalie* apologize!"

Me? I didn't hurt Laurie. Peter did.

"Natalie?" Miss Hines asks.

Laurie and Miss Hines turn and stare at me.

My stomach goes twitchy.

Miss Hines turns back to Peter. "Why should Natalie apologize?"

My heart is thumpy.

Peter puts his hands on his hips. "Because Natalie's the one who told me."

Chapter 9

Sticky Words

"You told Peter I have dyslexia?" Laurie says. Tears are dripping out of her eyes.

"No! Well, maybe. Kind of. But I didn't—"

"You?" Laurie won't let me get my words in. About how I didn't mean to tell Peter. And how *I* never made fun of her like Peter did. "I can't believe you'd do that to me, Nat."

"I–I—" Words are sticking to my neck.

I want to tell Laurie how it happened. I want to make her understand it was Peter's fault. I only just said that 'slexia word to make him stop calling her "dumb." I was sticking up for her.

But before my words get unstuck, Laurie runs to her desk.

I start to go after her. But Miss Hines sticks her arm out and stops me. "Wait, Natalie." She squats down between me and Peter. "Peter, you and I will have a little talk about this after school."

"That's not fair!" he whines.

"Take your seat, Peter."

Peter stomps back to his desk.

Miss Hines and I are still by the cubbies. Kids

are talking and laughing at each other. Plus, some kids are turning their heads to see what our teacher is doing with me back here.

Only Laurie has her head down on her desk. And some of the kids are staring at her.

"I didn't mean to tell Peter," I tell Miss Hines. "It just came out when I wasn't looking."

Miss Hines pushes her wire glasses up to her eyes. "Laurie's very upset, Natalie. She didn't want anyone to know about her business. And she had that right."

"I know."

"So why did you tell Peter?"

"'Cause he said Laurie was in the dumb group. And she's not dumb. And I wanted to make Peter take it back. And that word just popped out of me, even though I didn't want it to. And I only— "

Miss Hines stands up fast and points at Chase and Jason, on account of they are chasing each other around her desk. "Boys, sit down right now! Do you two want to miss recess again?"

Jason and Chase run fast to their desks.

"Everyone, get out your math workbooks, please." Miss Hines crosses the room to her big desk.

I figure I'm one of the *everyone* who needs to get out a math workbook. So I go to my desk. Only what

I really want is to go to Laurie's desk. On account of I want to tell her what really happened and how those words just came out of me 'cause I was so aggravated at Peter. I was sticking up for my bestest friend. That's what.

Miss Hines makes us copy numbers off her whiteboard. Laurie looks up to copy the numbers. I wave to her, but she doesn't see.

Sasha's desk is next to Laurie's. Sasha makes a frowny face back at me. Then she whispers something to Laurie.

The whole entire time we do math stuff, Laurie still won't look at me.

We put away our math papers. Then Miss Hines comes around and sits on the front of her desk. "Principal Fritz has set Friday as the date for our Kindergarten Olympics," she says. "That means we better get our teams together. We won't have much time to practice. So, could we have our team captains come to the front, please?"

Peter is already out of his seat. "Me first!" he shouts. "First picks!"

Miss Hines makes Peter stand on one side of her. "Laurie? Would you please come up to my desk so we can pick sides for our Olympic teams?"

Laurie shuffles to the other side of our teacher.

She stares at her shoes that are just like my shoes, kind of. As soon as Laurie picks me, I'll get to walk up and stand by her. And maybe I can whisper the stuff about Peter and about me sticking up for her. That should make her feel better. And me too.

"Since I pulled Peter's name from the hat first," Miss Hines explains, "he'll get to pick the first—"

"Yes!" Peter cries. "Me first!"

"Enough, Peter," Miss Hines says. "Unless you'd like Laurie to go first instead?"

I would like Laurie to go first instead, so I can be on her team for certain sure. That Peter is so not nice that he might pick me just to make Laurie and me sad.

Peter pretends to zip up his mouth. But when Miss Hines turns away, he sticks his we're-number-one finger in the air.

"All right, Peter. Go ahead," says our teacher.

My heart is thumpy. I grab on to the side of my desk to help.

"Carlo!" Peter yells.

Yes!

Carlo zips to the front to stand beside Peter. Carlo is a very fast running boy.

I let go of my desk and get ready to run my fastest to stand by Laurie.

Laurie looks up from her shoes. She is not smiley faced or frowny faced. Slowly, she turns her head, like she is looking at every kid in our classroom. When her eyes get to me, I smile. Only she doesn't. Her eyes keep going past me. And going. Until they stop on Sasha.

Then loud and clear, Laurie says, "Sasha."

Chapter 10

Un-Picked

Sasha?

Sasha? It's true that Sasha is a fast running girl. But she is also...Sasha. And she has been as not nice to us as Peter the Not-So-Great.

I think maybe I didn't hear right. My desk is in the way back of the room. Maybe Laurie said Natalie, and it sounded like Sasha.

Sasha jumps out of her seat and runs to the front of the classroom. She stops right next to Laurie.

My heart hurts. My seat is already out of my seat, and I have to put it back down. Why didn't Laurie pick me? She said she was going to. We *always* pick each other.

I try to remember exactly what Laurie said about our team. We talked about who else to get.

Maybe she didn't say she'd pick me first, even though it feels like a very sad thing not to be first.

Maybe Laurie is being a smart captain. On account of picking me first is a waste because I'm not so fast. So nobody else would want me on their team first. And Sasha *is* fast.

So maybe Laurie picked Sasha so Peter wouldn't get her. And she's sure Peter won't pick me.

I just hope she's right about that.

"Jason!" Peter yells.

Laurie and I wanted Jason on our team. Jason is a fast boy. Plus, he is a nice boy. For a boy. But at least Peter didn't pick me.

I wait for Laurie to say my name.

"Laurie?" Miss Hines says. "Your turn."

Sasha whispers something to Laurie.

"Chase," Laurie says.

My stomach goes from twitchy to twisty. I know Chase is a fast boy. But I still can't believe Laurie picked him before me.

"Rory," Peter says.

I am wishing that I could be a fast runner. I think about how Laurie wins every time we race. And I didn't even care before. Only I care now.

"Tosha," Laurie says.

Now I really don't get it. Tosha never runs. Sometimes.

Peter says a name that isn't me.

Laurie says a name that isn't me.

Peter says a name that isn't me.

Laurie says a name that isn't me.

I wish I could be home right now. And not here. I hate here.

When only four slow-running kindergartners are left, Jason says, "Pick Nat! Come on, Peter! Nat can run. Pick Nat!"

Peter scrunches up his face at me. Then he says, "Natalie, I guess."

I get up and walk to Peter's side. I watch my shoes and that's all.

"I am glad we are on this same team," Farah whispers when I get to the front. Peter picked her right before he picked me.

I try to smile back at Farah. But my smiley face has left kindergarten.

I take one secret look at Laurie and *her* team. She had a gazillion chances to pick me. She promised we'd be on the same team.

Laurie should have picked me. She didn't. And I will never ever never forget it. That's what.

Miss Hines sends us out to recess early. I don't run to the swings.

Farah walks up beside me. "Are you all right, Natalie?"

Part of me wants to say, "No! I'm very not all right. On account of my bestest friend didn't pick me. And I got picked almost last. And Laurie doesn't even care. And that makes my heart hurt with so much sad in there."

But some of that sad is changing into mad now. And that mad part of me wants to say, "Yes! I'm better than all right. Better 'cause I'm *not* going to be on Laurie's team. On account of she is a big traitor girl. That's what!"

"Natalie?" Farah sweeps her long hair behind her shoulders and gets big in her eyes. "Are you sick?"

I look up. And that's when I see that we are at the swings. Sasha and Laurie are swinging very high. I can tell without even asking that Laurie did not save me a swing.

And this turns the rest of the sad in me to mad.

I take Farah's arm and pull her away from the swings. But before we go, I say loud enough for Laurie to hear, "We don't want to swing, Farah. We need to find *our* team and be with them."

Jason and Peter are kicking a soccer ball at each other. I head for them, yelling, "We're number one! We're number one!"

And this yelling turns into a promise in my head. I'm going to do everything I can to beat Laurie and Sasha's team in the Kindergarten Olympics.

Chapter 11

Life after Laurie

Miss Hines gives us school time to meet with our teams. Peter's team gets one side of the classroom. Laurie's gets the other side. I try not to look at Laurie's team. Looking there makes the sad come back.

Peter is bossy. "*I'm* racing in the first race," he bosses. "Carlo can be in the long race." He gives out jobs like he is the boss of the world. Only not to Farah and me.

"What races are for Natalie and me?" Farah asks.

"I don't know," Peter answers. "You can cheer or something. I want to win."

Miss Hines has sneaked up to listen to Peter's team. She comes all the way over for this one. "Peter, I told you that everyone on your team will compete in at least one event. You should have plenty of openings for Farah and Natalie."

"I do not mind," Farah says.

"Well, I do," Miss Hines says. "Now, who's running in the first event?"

"Brandon and me," Peter says.

"All right. Who's in the second event?" asks our teacher.

"Carlo and me," Peter says.

"Then how about the shot-put throw?"

"Me and Bethany," Peter says.

Miss Hines gives Peter her line eyes. "Peter, you can't compete in every event. Pick two. That's it."

Peter kicks the floor.

Our teacher smiles at Farah. "Farah, I think you would be perfect for the shot put. All you do is throw a special ball as far as you can."

"But I—" Peter protests.

"Two events only, Peter," Miss Hines reminds him. She smiles at Farah again. "How about if you and Bethany do the shot put together?"

"Yes," Farah says.

"What about the hurdles?" Miss Hines asks.

"I want to do that one!" Peter shouts.

Miss Hines lets out a big, fat sigh. "Fine. You and Natalie can run hurdles. And that takes care of everybody, right?" She looks over at me. "Is that all right with you, Natalie?"

"I don't care," I say. But I don't know what running "hurls" means. I know what *hurling* means, on account of I do that when I'm stomach sick. But I never saw that one on the TV Olympics.

School gets over. For the first time forever, Laurie and I don't walk out together. This makes my heart hurt again. But I act like it doesn't. I make my feet skip on the sidewalk. I am a good skipping girl. Sometimes.

My feet skip all the way to Buddy. Only my heart doesn't. Before I get in, I look back and see Laurie getting into her mom's car. Laurie looks over at Buddy. I can see Laurie seeing me. Now is when we always wave at each other.

Only this time we don't.

Granny is sitting down in our front yard when Mom and I drive up in Buddy. She's digging in the dirt. If I didn't feel so sad and mad already, I would laugh at my granny.

"Hey, Nat!" Granny calls. "I could sure use some help planting these flowers."

"Please help your granny, Nat," Mom whispers. "I have some business calls to make." Mom is the flower planter in our house, except for this time.

"Okay." I am thinking that there is nothing else to do. Nobody to play with. Nobody to call and ask to come over.

Granny hands me a little shovel that's as big as my hand. "Start digging, cowgirl," she says.

It feels a little good to *dig, dig, dig* in the dirt.

"You're not much of a talker today," Granny says. "How was school?"

"I don't know." I don't want to talk about being un-picked.

Granny doesn't say anything. But I feel her staring.

"So, Nat," Granny says. "Why don't you phone Laurie and see if she can come help us plant these flowers?" She reaches into her pocket and holds out her cell phone.

"No, thanks." I keep on *dig, dig, digging*.

"Why not?"

"I don't want to. That's what."

Granny is quiet for minute. But not for long. "Nat, did you and Laurie have a fight?"

I stop digging. Laurie and I have never had a fight. Peter and I have. Sasha and I have. Even Granny and I have. Not Laurie and me. "We didn't yell at each other." In those other fights, there was a lot of that yelling going on.

Granny's eyes have sad in them. "Some fights don't come with yelling, Nat."

Chapter 12

Hurling Secrets

Beep! Beep!

A big black car drives into our driveway. My daddy gets out. The car belongs to Daddy's boss, who goes by the name of Mr. Adams. He and Daddy and another guy car pool to work. And that isn't fun like it sounds. There's no swimming in a car pool.

I run up to my dad. He lifts me high and spins me around. And I kind of wish he would stay holding on. But he puts me down and tells his boss good-bye.

"Nat," Daddy says when the black car drives away, "what's the latest on the Kindergarten Olympics?"

My stomach feels twitchy just at the sound of that word. "They happen on Friday."

"Friday? That doesn't give us much time to practice, does it? What's your event?"

"Hurling."

"Hurling? Like the sport they play in Ireland? Why would they make kindergartners learn hurling? I don't even think it's an Olympic event. Are you sure that's your event, Nat?"

"Miss Hines made Peter let me be the one to run

those hurls with him," I explain.

"Run those hurls? *Hurdles!* Is that what you mean, Nat? Are you running hurdles?" Daddy is really excited about this. "*I* ran hurdles in high school!"

After dinner, Daddy hurries me out to the backyard to practice hurling. It turns out hurdles are like little fences you jump over. I even saw those things on the TV Olympics.

"I don't suppose you know how high your hurdles will be, do you?" He's hammering nails into skinny boards. "No. Of course you don't. We'll just make different kinds of hurdles and different sizes, so you'll be ready for anything."

We pull out boards and empty boxes and build things to jump over. Daddy moves a yellow tube thing that Laurie and I crawl in and pretend it's a tunnel. Thinking about this makes my sadness come back. But I try to push it out with mad and remember how Laurie didn't pick me for her team.

By the time Daddy finishes our hurdles, the sun is dropping down in the sky.

"Nat, why don't you just run and jump over our hurdles to start out. Okay? Then we'll work on style."

"I'm not very fast," I warn him.

"You're plenty fast," Daddy says. "And hurdles are as much about jumping as running. You're a good jumper."

"I am?"

"Sure you are!" Daddy says. "How many times have you gotten in trouble for running up the hall and jumping over my footstool?"

This is a true thing. "Many times," I admit.

"On your mark!" he shouts. "Get set! Go!"

I run to the yellow tunnel, stop, jump, and run again. Then I do the same on the other two jumps. "I did it!" I cry.

"You sure did!" Daddy yells. "Not bad for a first try."

I walk over to Daddy. "But I wasn't very fast, was I?"

"You were fine. But let's do it again. Try the yellow jump. But this time, don't stop before you jump. Just keep on going. Lean forward, jump, and keep running."

"I'll try," I say. I take a big breath and run to the tunnel. I slow down, but I don't stop.

"Great!" Daddy shouts.

It feels a little great too, to have my dad say this. "Can I do it again?"

Mom comes out to watch. She sits on the swing, and I do all of the jumps again. And again. And this last time, I don't even slow down before I jump.

"You're a natural, Nat!" Mom says.

"She gets it from me," Daddy says, like he's proud about this. "Nat, come over here!" I do. "I'm going to tell you a secret, Nat. It's something my high school coach taught me. It's the reason I made it to State my senior year."

"What's the secret?" I ask.

Daddy looks over his shoulder like he wants to make sure nobody else can hear. Then he whispers, "Look at your watch when you sail over the jump."

This is not sounding like a very good secret to me. "Daddy, I don't have a watch."

"Look where your watch would be, on your wrist. That's how you make sure your arms are in the right place when you jump. Go on, Nat. Try it."

I try it. Only I forget the watch part. I do it again. This time I think about the watch I don't have. And I look.

"That's it, Nat!" Daddy shouts. "Keep going!"

I keep running to the next jump. This time I feel like I'm flying over that hurdle. When I look at where my watch isn't, I feel fast. That's what.

Mom and Dad clap for me when we quit. This feels like a happy thing.

I am still happy when I jump into my bubble bath. Only when I lean back, I see purple wallpaper. We have boring black-and-white wallpaper in here, except for where I'm looking. It's purple, on account of Laurie and I colored it that way one day before my mom made us stop.

By the time the bubbles are gone, so is my happy feeling.

I get in my jammies and still have a little time to play before bedtime. I pull out all of my stuffed animals and pretend I'm choosing up teams.

"Steg-O," I say, moving my dinosaur to one side. But my bear and my moose and my bunny and all the others look too sad. So I change my mind and scoop all of them to my side. "I pick all of you," I tell them. "On account of I don't ever want you guys to feel un-picked."

Chapter 13

How Did the Hamster Cross the Road?

I wake up and get ready for school, and it's still dark outside. Percy stays sleeping on my bed.

"Percy," I tell my sleepyhead cat, "maybe Laurie will get to school early. And maybe she will see me. And she will say, 'Nat, I'm really sorry I didn't pick you for my Olympic team.' And I will say, 'Laurie, I'm really sorry about spilling your 'slexia secret.' And then I'll have my bestest friend back."

And I think this might be a true thing about today. On account of I thought about this thing all night.

I change my purple shirt to the pink shirt that Laurie has one just like.

"You're ready for school already?" Mom asks when I come out to the kitchen.

She is not ready for anything. She's sitting at the table in her blue fuzzy robe and green slippers.

"Can we go to school now?" I ask.

Mom sets down her coffee mug. "Don't you think we should eat breakfast first?"

I don't think this. But she makes me anyway.

The phone rings, and Mom runs to answer it. She is still not in real clothes.

"Morning, my little hurdler!" Daddy shuffles into the kitchen in his torn-up slippers that he won't let Mom throw away. He still has sleepy eyes.

"Morning, Daddy."

He pours his coffee and sits down with me. I can hear Mom talk-talk-talking in the living room.

"Tomorrow's the big day, huh?" Daddy asks.

I feel like *today* is the big day. But I know he means the Olympics day. "Yep."

"I imagine you'll get time to practice today, though. Just remember. No stopping. And check your watch."

"Got it." I wish Mom would come. I want to get to school.

"You're going to blow them away, Nat," Daddy says. He takes the newspaper Mom was reading and goes to a different page.

I wait a gazillion minutes.

Mom sticks her head in. She is still in her robe. "Sorry, Nat! I'll run and get dressed. We won't be late to school. I promise."

Mom keeps her promise. We're not late. But we're not early. Kids are pouring into my school when I walk up the sidewalk.

I don't see Laurie until I get inside the school. She and Sasha are talking outside the door of my

classroom. Sasha looks up at me. Then she pulls
Laurie into our room.

When I walk into our room, Sasha and Laurie are
laughing by the cubbies. I don't want to go where
they are together. Only I have to hang up my jacket.

"Jason says you're running in the hurdles race,"
Sasha says.

I don't answer, on account of it isn't a question.

"You might as well drop out now," Sasha says.
"Laurie and I are both running in that race."

This feels like a not fair thing, but I don't know
why. Plus, the sad in me is turning back to mad.
"So?" I say, wiggling out of my jacket.

"So, we beat you to the swings every single day,"
Sasha says. She has laughing in her voice.

"Well, we don't jump over the swings." I reach
up my jacket and hang it on the hook in my cubby.
Only Laurie's jacket is hogging up room. *Her* sleeve
is in *my* cubby. I shove it back where it belongs.

"Hey!" Laurie shouts. "Leave my jacket alone."

I turn my line eyes at her. "Then keep it in *your*
cubby!"

"Come on, Laurie," Sasha says. She takes
Laurie's hand. "Let's go talk about *our* team plans."

I watch them walk away together to their desks.
My stomach is twitchy, and my neck is chokey. And

I want to go home.

Jason runs by me. Then he runs backwards, back to me. "Hey, Nat! Did you tell Ham a joke yet?"

I shake my head. Almost every day, I tell our class pet, Ham the Hamster, a joke I make up. But I don't feel jokey today.

"Come on, Nat!" Jason begs. He loves my hamster jokes.

I look over at Sasha and Laurie. They're laughing. And it feels like they are laughing at me.

Fine, I say to myself.

I follow Jason to the hamster cage. Ham *scritch-scratches* his way over to me for his joke. "Go on, Nat!" Jason says.

"How did the hamster cross the road?" I ask. This is almost how I start all the jokes. Only I usually ask *why* Ham crossed the road, instead of *how*.

"I don't know," Jason says. "How did the hamster cross the road?"

"By jumping way high over hurdles and winning the Kindergarten Olympics and beating the other team. That's what."

Chapter 14

Bad Team Spirit

The only real school we do in the morning is reading. But we are more like bumbly bees than birds in our groups 'cause kids are excited about the Olympics.

"Boys and girls?" Miss Hines taps her desk to make us quiet. "We're going outside now to practice our Olympic events. Our principal will lead Peter's team to the track. I'll take Laurie's team on the north side of the building. Then we'll trade places, so Laurie's team can use the track. Line up!"

"Me first!" Peter cries.

"And don't forget!" Miss Hines shouts. "The other kindergarten class has teams there too. They should be just about finished with their practice, I think. Let's be good sports, though. I want good team spirit."

I line up with Peter's team. Farah and I are the very last in the line. Principal Fritz comes to lead us outside. We are very quiet, on account of she can be scary when she wants to. Right now, she isn't. She has frizzy black hair, black glasses, and a black jogging suit.

We pass the other kindergarten class on our way to the field. They make faces at us, and we make faces at them.

Peter breaks out of line when we get close to the track. Carlo runs after him, and Jason passes them both.

Principal Fritz blows her whistle at them. "I want everyone over there by the volunteers. First-race runners, line up now."

Peter runs to the beginning line. "Me first!" he shouts. Peter did what Miss Hines made him do and put everyone on his team in a race. Only he and Jason still ended up with two races.

In the first race, Peter is running with Julia. She was the very last person chosen in our kindergarten class. Julia takes tiny steps to the beginning line. She is way wider and bigger than Peter, only maybe the same tallness.

Principal Fritz shouts into a funnel thing, "On your mark! Get set! Go!"

Peter jumps ahead and keeps getting more and more ahead. When he crosses the finish line, he shouts, "I won! I won! Me first!"

We wait for Julia to get here too. I guess she's running, but it might be walking. Principal Fritz cheers for Julia when she's finished racing.

There are more races. Jason wins both of his. He doesn't even shout, "Me first." But he keeps running when he crosses the finish line 'cause the run isn't all out of him yet.

Bethany and Farah have to throw big brown balls. Farah's ball goes way farther than Bethany's.

I run up to Farah. "Wow! You're a great ball thrower!"

Farah smiles without her teeth. "Thank you, Natalie." She turns to Bethany and shakes her hand. "I like your throw as well," she says.

Principal Fritz hollers at the grown-up helpers, "Volunteers, please set up our hurdles!"

"That means me and you, Natalie Lizard Breath," Peter says.

I pretend I don't hear Peter. On account of my name being Natalie 24 and only sometimes Natalie Elizabeth. But nobody ever calls me Natalie Lizard

Breath, except for Peter the Not-So-Great. And maybe sometimes Sasha the Not-So-Nice.

I can see three hurdles set up on our running circle. They are all way shorter than the jumps in my backyard. Shorter is easier. My heart is a little thumpy in a good way.

"Good luck, Natalie," Farah says.

I move to the start line. Peter lines up next to me. He scoots his toes as close as he can to the line.

"I'm going to beat you bad, Lizard Breath!" Peter says.

Principal Fritz calls over, "Don't forget, you're on the same team! Let's see some team spirit!"

Peter growls. He has team spirit, but it's all bad. That's what.

"On your mark!" shouts Principal Fritz. "Get set! Go!"

Peter is a very fast boy and gets way ahead of me. Only when he gets to the first hurdle, Peter stops, jumps, and starts running again.

I keep on running, jump, and keep running. And I'm almost up with Peter, on account of I didn't stop.

Peter frowns at me over his shoulder. He's not far ahead of me. But now he runs even faster. I run the same fastness as I did.

We get to the next hurdle. Peter stops. But I keep

running, jump, and run more.

"Hey! You can't pass me!" Peter yells.

But I'm still running. When I get to the next hurdle, I do my running jump. And this time, I remember to look at my watch I don't have. I am a flying girl.

I run across the finish line. Jason and Farah are there, cheering their heads off.

"You won!" Farah shouts.

Jason yells, "Nat's number one! Nat's number one!"

Peter stomps up to us. "No fair! I'm faster than you are!" He yells over at Principal Fritz, "I don't want to do that race! I want to run in a different race!"

"Too bad!" Principal Fritz hollers.

My heart is thumpy. I won. I beat Peter.

And there is another thing in my head. This thought makes me want it to be the real Kindergarten Olympics and not just practice. I want to beat Peter again.

Plus, I want to beat more than just Peter. I want to beat Sasha.

And Laurie. That's what.

Chapter 15

Digging

Lunch is not as much fun as it usually is. I sit at one table with Farah and Anna. Laurie sits at another table with Sasha and Bethany. Nobody trades half of her sandwich with me. Plus, I can see Laurie. And she takes a giant piece of cake from Sasha's lunch.

"What is wrong with you and Laurie?" Farah asks.

This question makes my sandwich stop going down my neck. So I can't get an answer out.

"They're not friends anymore," Anna says.

I choke down my bite of sandwich. "What?"

"That's what Sasha said," Anna says.

"She said Laurie and I aren't friends? Not just not bestest friends? Not any kind of friends?"

"Sasha told Bethany and me that she and Laurie are best friends, and you and Laurie aren't even speaking-to-each-other friends," Anna says.

I put my sandwich back in my lunch box. On account of I'm not hungry anymore. Plus, my stomach hurts. And other things inside of me hurt too.

Granny picks me up from school in her car, which

goes by the name of Charlotte the Chevrolet. She takes me back to her house to plant flowers there.

I *dig, dig, dig* where Granny shows me to by her front step. Only this is not so much fun as you think it is.

Granny is humming a church song that goes by the name of "What a Friend We Have in Jesus." I can't help having these words in my head while she hums. It feels part good, on account of I know I have one friend. And part bad, on account of that's all.

"Okay, kid. What's up?" Granny has sneaked over to sit on her step.

"I'm digging," I tell her.

She takes my little shovel from my hand. "Are you and Laurie still at odds?"

I stare at the hole I made in the dirt. "Laurie didn't pick me to be on her Olympic team."

"Well, you can't always pick who you want if—"

"She could! Laurie was a team captain. She didn't pick me first. Then she didn't pick me again. And again. And again." I stop 'cause my neck is too chokey to keep going.

"I see," Granny says.

"And it hurt my feelings really bad. And she should say sorry to me." Tears start leaking out of me.

"I can see why you're so upset," Granny says.

"Plus, Laurie only talks to Sasha. And eats her cake. And they laugh together without me."

"Hmmm," Granny says. "That doesn't sound like the Laurie I know."

"Plus also, Laurie said she's not my friend anymore."

"Laurie said that?"

"Anna said that Sasha said Laurie said that," I explain.

"Hmmm," Granny says again. "Something tells me there's more to this story. Did you do something to make Laurie upset?"

"No!" I shout. "Well, maybe. Kind of."

Granny is quiet. But she's waiting. And she is a good waiter.

"You know how you said not to let anybody call Laurie's group dumb? Well, Peter did. So I told him not to. And he said Laurie was dumb. And I said, 'No, sir! Laurie's not dumb. She just has 'slexia.'"

"Ah. You told Peter this?"

"I didn't mean to, Granny."

"Laurie asked you not to tell anybody, didn't she?"

"But Peter—"

"But you did," Granny goes on. "And Peter probably told everybody, right?"

"He blabbed all over the place."

"Which he wouldn't have been able to do if you hadn't told him Laurie's secret in the first place," Granny finishes.

My head is running that whole horrible picture when I yelled to Peter that Laurie had 'slexia. And I don't like thinking about this part.

"Did you tell Laurie how sorry you are?" Granny asks.

"I tried! She won't even let me."

"How hard did you try, Nat?" Granny asks.

"Hard! Only Laurie only talks to Sasha."

Granny's face scrunches like she doesn't much like this answer.

"Laurie should say sorry for not picking me for her team!" I explain.

"Sounds to me like there's plenty of sorry to go around," Granny says.

"Well, she should go first!"

Granny laughs.

I cannot believe my Granny is doing this laugh. "It's not funny, Granny!"

"No, it's not," Granny agrees. "I was just thinking. I sat out in that schoolyard waiting for you this afternoon, and I must have heard a dozen kids yell, 'Me first!'"

I still don't get it. Kids yell this all the time. "So?"

"I was chuckling because everybody wants to be first, except when it comes to saying sorry."

I stare down at my hole in the dirt. It looks empty. And I think that's how I probably look on my insides. On account of that's how I feel. 'Cause I told Laurie's secret and didn't even tell her I was sorry. And empty 'cause I miss my bestest friend.

Granny goes back to planting and humming that song about having a friend in Jesus.

I close my eyes, and my tears splash into the dirt. Then I talk to my friend Jesus. And the first thing I say is *sorry*.

Chapter 16

Winners

Kindergarten Olympics day is sunny, with real birds singing in the trees. I can't wait to talk to Laurie. Even if she never tells me sorry, I want to tell her sorry.

When I get to my classroom, we are already divided up in teams. Laurie is too far away for me to talk to. Plus, she still won't look at me.

Miss Hines makes us line up in teams to go outside. "Now remember the spirit of the Olympics," she tells us. "Let's be good sports and have fun!"

Farah and I walk to the running circle together. On one side of the track, parents are already sitting on blankets and chairs.

"That is your grandmother, is it not?" Farah says, pointing.

I see her too. And Mommy and Daddy.

"Go, Nat!" Daddy yells. He keeps yelling this until I wave.

"Welcome to Kindergarten Olympics!" Principal Fritz shouts through her squeaky speaker.

It feels like a real Olympics. But it's hard to get excited about it until I talk to Laurie. And her team is too far away.

Kids from both kindergartens line up for the first race.

"On your mark! Get set! Go!" Principal Fritz yells.

Farah and I watch and cheer for our side. So many people scream that I can't hear my own scream. Andrew from the other kindergarten comes in first, and Peter next. Only Peter yells at everybody, 'cause he wanted to win first.

"Have you seen Laurie?" I ask Farah, while other kids get to the start line.

"She is still with her team." Farah points to the other team's waiting spot. Laurie is there, next to Sasha.

Farah and I watch more races. We scream our heads off.

"Who is the winner so far?" Farah asks.

"I don't know." Miss Hines told us about keeping score and every place getting points. Only I didn't get it.

Farah gets second place in her shot-put throw. Jason wins one of his races and comes in second in the other one. Then it's my turn.

"And now our last event!" Principal Fritz yells. "The hurdles!"

"That's you!" Farah says.

I move to the start line. I can hear my dad's cheering louder than anybody's. Plus also Granny's.

My stomach is very twitchy. All day, I have been twitchy about talking to Laurie. Now I am also twitchy about this race.

The other kindergarten takes up half of the line. Then Peter, Sasha, me, and Laurie. Laurie is the farthest-away girl.

"I can trade places with you if you want," I tell Laurie.

She gets big in her eyes.

"Stay where you are, Lizard Breath!" Peter yells. "Her spot has to run longer."

"I know," I tell him.

"I'm okay," Laurie says.

"Yeah," Sasha calls over. "We're just fine! We're going to win! We're number one!"

This sets Peter off. "*We're* number one!" he shouts.

I want to tell Laurie I'm sorry for everything. Only Peter and Sasha are too loud. Plus, I know we're not supposed to talk on the start line. But I've waited and waited to talk to her. And I can't wait more. "Laurie, I—"

"Quiet, please!" Principal Fritz yells. "On your mark! Get set! Go!"

My feet take off. But they are not super fast feet. Sasha, Peter, and Laurie get in front right away. They get to the first hurdle before me. But they all stop or slow way down.

I keep running. Jump. And run some more.

"Way to jump, Nat!" Daddy screams so loud, I hear him.

I'm right between Peter and Laurie now. We run. Only they move ahead of me.

We get to the next hurdle, and I fly over it, checking my watch I don't have. When I land, nobody is in front of me. I don't even hear footsteps behind me.

I keep running. Nobody is coming up on me.

I peek over my shoulder. Peter is back there.

"We're killing them!" Peter shouts. "Ha! Look how far back Laurie is!"

Close behind Peter comes Sasha. Laurie is behind her.

I keep peeking at Laurie. She is in the way back. I start running backwards to see her better. Her face is sad, and that makes me sorry in my heart. I don't want Laurie to be sad.

Sasha is running past Peter. I see this on account of I am still running backwards.

"Out of the way!" Sasha shouts. She runs right at me.

I try to turn frontwards. But Sasha bumps my shoulder and sends me smashing into the last hurdle. I bounce off and slam down on the track.

"Get up!" Peter shouts mean. He stops and jumps that hurdle.

Only I stay down.

"Nat, are you okay?" Laurie runs up and kneels beside me.

Tears leak out of me.

"You're hurt! I'll get your mom!" Laurie starts to get up.

I grab her arm. "I'm not hurt!" And this is a true thing. The tears aren't outside-hurt tears. They're inside-hurt tears. "I'm okay. I…I'm just sorry, Laurie."

Laurie's eyes get tears. "I'm sorry too, Nat. I—"

"No. Me first," I say. "I'm so sorry." It feels good to get out those words. "I never should have told your secret. I didn't mean to. I was trying to make Peter stop saying you were in the dumb group. Only I shouldn't have told him about the 'slexia. And now everybody knows. And it's all my fault. And now you don't even want to be my friend."

"What?" Laurie is big in her teary eyes. "Nat, I was just so sad that it turned into mad. And then I didn't pick you on my team. And I'm really sorry I didn't. But how could you think I don't want to be your friend?"

"Anna said Sasha said you didn't," I explain.

"Sasha told *me* you said *you* didn't want to be my friend. You didn't want a friend with dyslexia."

"I *never* said that! I always want you to be—!"

"Run!" Peter stands over me. "If you beat Laurie, we can still win!" he screams.

Sasha runs up to Laurie. "Laurie! All you have to do is finish the race before Nat! Go!"

"Get going, Lizard Breath!" Peter yells.

Sasha mean-laughs.

Laurie jumps to her feet. I think she may be going

to finish the race. But she doesn't jump the hurdle.
She turns line eyes at Sasha and Peter. "Don't call
Nat 'Lizard Breath'! Don't you ever say that name to
my bestest friend again!"

Bestest friend. Those are the bestest words I have
ever heard. That's what.

"Come on, Nat." Laurie sticks out her hand and
helps me stand up.

My knee is scraped, but I don't hurt. Not outside.
And not inside.

Laurie and I hold hands and jump the hurdle
together. Then we run, laughing, to the finish line
and step on it at the exactly same time.

And guess what. We are both winners.